ÉGALITÈ

Daniela and the Pirate Girls
Egalité Series

© Text: Susanna Isern, 2019
© Illustrations: Gómez, 2019
© Edition: NubeOcho, 2020
© Translation: Laura Victoria Fielden, 2020
www.nubeocho.com · hello@nubeocho.com

Original title: *Daniela y las chicas pirata*
Text editing: Cecilia Ross and Rebecca Packard

First edition: May 2020
ISBN: 978-84-17673-27-7
Legal deposit: M-19649-2019

Printed in Portugal.

DANIELA

AND THE PIRATE GIRLS

SUSANNA ISERN
& GÓMEZ

nubeOCHO

ON A FARAWAY SEA sailed the *Black Croc*, the most fearsome pirate ship of all time.

DANIELA was its captain.

One day, while sailing the South Seas,
A CROW flew by carrying a message in its beak.

WE ARE TRAPPED IN
A CAVE. FOLLOW OUR
SONG AND RESCUE US.

—THE MERGIRLS AND MERBOYS

The pirates went quiet, and they could hear **THE SONG OF THE MERFOLK** in the distance. They followed it until they came to a huge **GRAY ROCK**.

Without thinking twice, Daniela and her crew DOVE INTO THE OCEAN.

They swam and swam, until they arrived at the cave of
THE MERGIRLS AND MERBOYS!

When they arrived, they found the merfolk SINGING HAPPILY.

"We've come to help!" said Daniela.

"Thanks a lot, but the FEARLESS PIRANHAS have already saved us!"

The mermaids told them that the Fearless Piranhas were a group of girls who sailed aboard an ENORMOUS SHIP. They had never seen pirates SO BRAVE!

"We have to find these Fearless Piranhas!" said Daniela. "I want to see
WITH MY OWN TWO EYES if they're really as amazing as they sound."

The *Black Croc* set off in search of the
Fearless Piranhas. Along the way,
they ran into A SUBMARINE.

"Has a ship of PIRATE GIRLS been
through here?" asked Daniela.

"Yes! We were cornered at the bottom of the
sea by DANGEROUS SHARKS, but thanks
to them, we managed to escape."

The *Black Croc* sailed on and came upon A GIGANTIC WHALE.

"You look happy, whale," said Daniela.

"I am! I was beached for days. Nobody was able to help me get back into the water. But then these fantastic pirate girls showed up, and they RESCUED ME!"

Daniela and her crew sailed on towards THE VOLCANIC ISLAND.
As they approached, Daniela saw through the spyglass a ship anchored offshore.

"No way! What if they find THE TREASURE?" asked a worried Daniela.
The lost treasure that the *Black Croc* had spent ages searching for was buried there.

When they got off the ship, they found that the Fearless Piranhas had already left.

"Those girls are INCREDIBLE! They helped us cover the volcano so the lava wouldn't reach the village," said an old man. "To thank them, we told them where the treasure is BURIED."

"NOOO!" Daniela and her crew exclaimed sadly.

Daniela and the *Black Croc* pirates couldn't believe it! The Fearless Piranhas were suddenly FAMOUS and making off with all the BEST TREASURE.

"We have to find them! Tack north, me hearties!" shouted Daniela.

In the distance, they saw A TERRIBLE STORM approaching. But if the Fearless Piranhas weren't afraid, then they weren't either!

The *Black Croc* sailed into the storm and finally caught sight of
the Fearless Piranhas' ship.

Just then, a HUGE WAVE crashed into the Fearless Piranhas' vessel,
and all the pirates aboard it were tossed into the water.

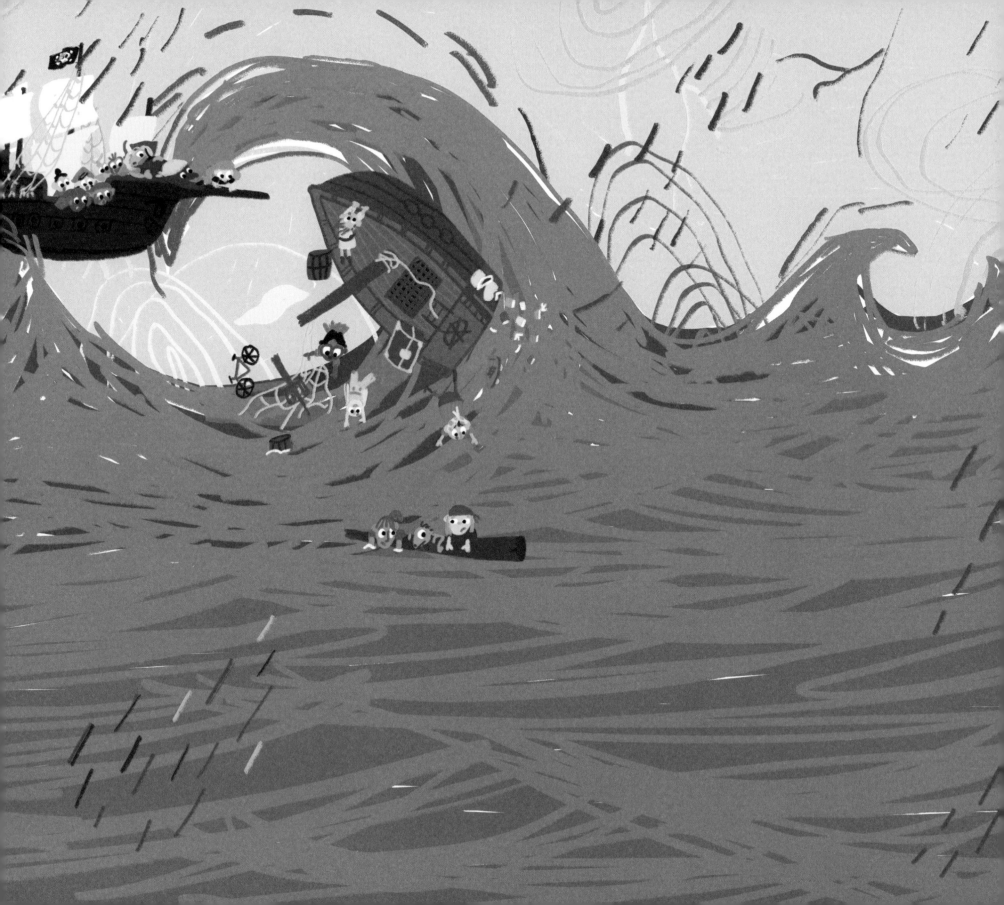

Without batting an eyelid, Daniela and her crew drew closer to rescue them.

"I know someone who can help us," said Daniela.

The captain began to WHISTLE with all her might. Instantly, THE WHALE they had met earlier burst from the waves.

Despite the storm, Daniela and her crew jumped onto the whale's back
and helped the pirate girls clamber to safety.

One by one, **THEY RESCUED THEM ALL**.

The whale dropped everyone off at the *Black Croc,* far from the storm.
Then it pushed the pirate girls' DAMAGED SHIP alongside them.

"I'm **ZOE, THE CAPTAIN** of the Fearless Piranhas. Thanks for rescuing us!"

"Do you and your crew want to stay aboard the *Black Croc* while your ship is being repaired?" asked Daniela.

"Really? We thought YOU DIDN'T LIKE US."

"We were a little annoyed that you were always one step ahead of us, but the Fearless Piranhas are amazing!" replied Daniela.

"Two ships and two captains make A GREAT TEAM," said Captain Zoe.

LONG LIVE THE CAPTAINS!

After a few weeks of work, the pirate girls' ship was fixed. The *Black Croc* and the Fearless Piranhas sailed off together on that faraway sea.

They had
AMAZING ADVENTURES.

But... what happened to the
VOLCANIC ISLAND TREASURE?

The Fearless Piranhas shared it to show their gratitude.

LONG LIVE THE PIRATE GIRLS!